Shen Roddie was born in Singapore. She graduated with a degree in history and began her career as a journalist, interviewing the first men to land on the moon. She lived in Buenos Aires, Argentina and Holland before settling back in Oxford. Shen's previous books include *Mrs Wolf!* (Tango), which was shortlisted for the Sheffield Libraries Book Award, *Shipwreck!* and *Fancy That!* (Victoria House), *Henry's Box* (Ladybird) and, for Frances Lincoln, *Toes are to Tickle*.

Sally Anne Lambert grew up in Crosby, Liverpool. Her first book, *The Ginger Bread Man* (Pavilion), was commissioned while she was still a student at Lanchester University, Coventry, where she graduated with a BA Hons in graphic design. Her previous titles include *Time for Bed* and *Hungry Bear* (Heinemann), *Three Little Pigs* (Ladybird), *Leon's Fancy Dress Day* (Macdonald) and, for Frances Lincoln, *Hippety-hop, Hippety-hay* with Opal Dunn.

Shen Roddie and Sally Anne Lambert have previously collaborated on *Best of Friends* (Frances Lincoln), the story of Hippo and Pig who discover that even best friends need their privacy.

For my sisters, with love ~ S.R.
For Jonny and Katie ~ S.A.L.

First published in Great Britain in 2000 by
Frances Lincoln Limited, 4 Torriano Mews,
Torriano Avenue, London NW5 2RZ

First paperback edition 2001

British Library Cataloguing in Publication Data available on request

ISBN 0-7112-1529-4 hardback
ISBN 0-7112-1532-4 paperback

Printed in Hong Kong

3 5 7 9 8 6 4 2

'SIMON SAYS!'

Shen Roddie 🖊 Sally Anne Lambert

FRANCES LINCOLN

Simon Pig was digging in his garden
when along came Sally Goose, on her way
to the Giant Melon Fair.

"Ooh! Ouch! This is hard work!"
grumbled Simon.

"Why don't you make a game of it?"
asked Sally Goose. "Then it will be fun!"

"Good idea!" cried Simon. "Let's play Simon Says!
You do whatever Simon Says. But when I say
'Sally Says', you must stand still.
If you don't, you're out!" said Simon.
"That's easy!" said Sally Goose.

So Simon said:

"Simon Says dig a hole and plant a carrot!"

Sally dug a hole and planted a carrot.
She was very pleased.
"Great game!" said Sally Goose.

"Simon Says make a scarecrow
and stick him in!"

Sally made a flappity scarecrow
and stuck him in.
"This is fun!" she said.

"Simon Says go upstairs and run the bath!"

Sally ran into the house and up the stairs.

She turned on the tap and ran Simon a bubbly bath.

"Simon Says scrub my back and clip my nails!"
said Simon.

"Ugh! What a dirty pig," Sally thought,
as she scrubbed and clipped.

"Simon Says wash the dishes and stack them up!"
Sally washed a whole week's dishes and stacked
them all up.

"This game is tiring me out!" said Sally Goose.
"Can I have a cup of tea now?"
"No. You don't want tea," said Simon.
"You're doing very well. Keep it up."

Simon carried on:
"Simon Says bake a cake and make a jelly."

Sally Goose groaned.
She baked a cake...

and made a jelly.

"When are you going to say 'Sally Says'?"
asked Sally. "I need a break!"

"Can't tell you, can I?" said Simon.
"I need to catch you out!"

"Well, you won't," thought Sally.
"I'm not such a silly goose. I won't be caught out.
You'll see!"

"Simon Says make me a wig and sew me a waistcoat."

Sally made him a wig and sewed him a waistcoat.

"Aren't I gorgeous!" said Simon, admiring himself
in the mirror.

"Not a bit, bully Pig!" said Sally, half collapsing
on the floor.

"Simon Says knit me a hammock and swing me to sleep!"

Sally knitted a knobbly hammock and swung him to sleep.

"Hurray!" said Sally when Simon began to snore. "I'm off!"

But just as Sally shut the gate, Simon jumped up and said, "Sally says leave the garden and shut the gate! There!" said Simon. "You've left the garden and shut the gate! You've done what Sally Says. You're not supposed to do that! You should be standing still!"

"You're out, Sally Goose!" yelled Simon.
"I'm not playing!" Sally yelled back.
"Not unless I have a go!"
"Oh, all right, then," said Simon.
"You can have a go. But only one
or you'll be late for your fair!"

Sally Goose smiled.

"Well then," said Sally Goose. "Simon Says give Sally and her melon a piggyride all the way to the fair!

And make it QUICK..."

And Simon did!

OTHER PICTURE BOOKS IN PAPERBACK
FROM FRANCES LINCOLN

BEST OF FRIENDS
Shen Roddie
Illustrated by Sally Anne Lambert

Hippo and Pig are neighbours and great friends, until one day Hippo decides to cut down the hedge so they can see into each other's homes.

Suitable for National Curriculum English – Reading, Key Stage 1
Scottish Guidelines English Language – Reading, Levels A and B

ISBN 0-7112-1226-0

TOES ARE TO TICKLE
Shen Roddie
Illustrated by Kady MacDonald Denton

'A puddle is to jump in. A handbag is to empty.' Children's first discoveries about the world around them are expressed with humour and sensitivity in this delightful book.

Suitable for Nursery Level; and for National Curriculum English – Reading, Key Stage 1
Scottish Guidelines English Language – Reading, Level A

ISBN 0-7112-1112-4

LITTLE BROTHER AND THE COUGH
Hiawyn Oram
Illustrated by Mary Rees

Meeting your new baby brother for the first time is not easy. In this case, it leads to a Cough, a very very VERY Bad Cough!

Suitable for National Curriculum English – Reading, Key Stages 1 and 2
Scottish Guidelines English Language – Reading, Level A

ISBN 0-7112-0845-X

Frances Lincoln titles are available from all good bookshops.